Praise for Storyshares

"One of the brightest innovators and game-changers in the education industry."
— Forbes

"Your success in applying research-validated practices to promote literacy serves as a valuable model for other organizations seeking to create evidence-based literacy programs."
— Library of Congress

"We need powerful social and educational innovation, and Storyshares is breaking new ground. The organization addresses critical problems facing our students and teachers. I am excited about the strategies it brings to the collective work of making sure every student has an equal chance in life."
— Teach For America

"It's the perfect idea. There's really nothing like this. I mean, wow, this will be a wonderful experience for young people."
— Andrea Davis Pinkney, Executive Director, Scholastic

"Reading for meaning opens opportunities for a lifetime of learning. Providing emerging readers with engaging texts that are designed to offer both challenges and support for each individual will improve their lives for years to come. Storyshares is a wonderful start."
— David Rose, Co-founder of CAST & UDL

The Mystery History

Storyshares presents

Published by Storyshares, LLC
Inspiring reading with a new kind of book.

Storyshares
Storyshares, LLC
24 N. Bryn Mawr Avenue #340
Bryn Mawr, Pennsylvania 19010-3304
www.storyshares.org

Interest Level: Middle School
Grade Level Equivalent: 4.1

ISBN 9798885977609
Book design by Saskia Globig

The Mystery History

The Market at Night #2

Cat Jenkins

Storyshares

Chapter 1

Have you ever noticed that there are two kinds of secrets?

First, there's the kind that are hard to keep. You want to tell someone because the secret is too big or maybe too scary for one person.

Then, there's the kind that you want to hug to yourself because it makes you feel special. Like a treasure that is all yours until you decide to share it.

That kind of secret can make you smile every time you think of it.

That kind of secret... the treasure kind... is what Angela had.

Chapter 2

Angela rolled the little bottle from Adam Zimmerman's Rewind Shop between her fingers.

She held it up to the light streaming through her bedroom window. Closing one eye, she squinted at the little bottle.

The sunlight broke into bars of color as it passed through the glass, painting a rainbow on Angela's bedroom wall.

The wall-rainbow was pretty, but it couldn't compare to the first time she'd seen the bottle. Mr. Adam Zimmerman, owner of Adam Zimmerman's Rewind Shop, had given it to her. The colors swirling inside the bottle had amazed her.

It had been three days… and nights!… since Angela's adventure in Seattle's Pike Place Market. She was still having trouble believing the world of magical strangeness she had found there. Magic seemed to take over the Market at night.
And she was already planning her return.

The only thing that bothered Angela was that she hadn't told anyone about it. Not even her best friend, Mindy.

She wasn't sure why, but every time she was about to tell anyone, something stopped her.

The words sat on the tip of her tongue. That's where they remained. Unspoken.

So the Market at night stayed Angela's secret treasure. It made her smile when she thought of it.

She couldn't wait to go back.

Chapter 3

"You wanna come over and study tonight?"

She and Mindy were sitting at a table in the school cafeteria. Mindy was poking at the salad she'd brought for lunch.

She made the invitation sound like anything but fun.

Angela frowned as she unwrapped the sandwich she'd brought for her own meal. "Study?"

"Yeah. History. You wanna?"

Angela's frown deepened. "History."

"We have that test. Local history. Remember?" Mindy stabbed a cherry tomato with her fork, taking out her dislike of tests on the poor vegetable.

She popped the wounded tomato into her mouth and chewed. "What's with you, Angie? Last few days it's like you're on another planet or something. Anyway, Nana Ree's gonna visit some friends, so I'll be pretty much alone until late. Be kind of nice to have someone over."

Angela had only been half-listening. Most of her mind had been on Pike Place Market and how she really wanted to go back. How she wanted to see if it was all still there.

The after-dark Market, that is. Not the every-day, normal Market. That Market was wonderful, of course. But it wasn't the night Market.

Mindy and her grandmother, Nana Ree, lived in one of the apartments in the Market offered to disabled senior artists in the Seattle community.

And that apartment was across the street from the shop with the neon green eye in the window.

And that was the shop that contained the entrance to the mystical, magical, marvelous night-time Market.

And it would be so easy for Angela to tell her parents she was studying with Mindy and staying the night.

And it would be so easy to sneak out when Mindy and Nana were asleep...

And why couldn't she just tell Mindy that?

But the words stuck on the tip of Angela's tongue. The only words that were allowed to pass were, "Sure, Min. I kinda forgot about the test. And I really need to study. Maybe I could even spend the night?"

Chapter 4

So that's how Angela found herself lying on her back at the foot of Mindy's bed. She had a history book propped open and resting on her chest.

Mindy was focused on Seattle's history. But Angela's mind was still on Pike Place Market, just outside and across the street.

"Angie!"

"Hmmm?"

Angela was wondering how long before Mindy's grandmother returned. She'd have to wait until both Mindy and Nana Ree were asleep before she could sneak out.

If only Mindy weren't so determined to… you know… study.

Mindy tapped a finger on her laptop screen. "I know this'll be on the test tomorrow: What was Seattle called when pioneers first settled here?"

"Huh?" Angela tried to pull her eyes away from the darkening sky outside the window.

Vendors and performers would be putting the daytime Market to bed.

But the nighttime Market should be waking up.

If it were real.

If I didn't dream the whole thing…

Chapter 5

"C'mon!" Mindy's voice had an edge of impatience. "The test is tomorrow! What. Was. Seattle. Called. Before. It was. Seattle?"

"Oh, uh…" Angela pulled her gaze away from the twilight seeping into the Seattle sky. "I know this… uh… It was called 'New York,' believe it or not. Right?"

Mindy laughed. "Right! Wouldn't that have been wild? Two New Yorks?"

Angela grinned and for a moment she let thoughts of the Market slip away. "That would have been really confusing. I'm glad they let Seattle have its own name."

"Well, they didn't change it right away. They

made it New York-Alki for a while," Mindy said.

"Oh, yeah! I remember."

But even as she said it, Angela's eyes drifted back toward the window. Daylight had been replaced by the gentle glow of city streetlamps.

Mindy carried on with her review for tomorrow's exam.

"Yeah. They tacked on 'alki,' 'cause it means 'by and by.' Guess they figured, in time, the town would grow big enough to rival New York #1. So, New York-Alki. From one of the local tribes."

Mindy wrinkled her nose, concentrating. "Duwamish? Was that the tribe?... Angie! Was it Duwamish?"

"Uh, yeah. I think so. And then they changed it to Seattle in honor of the native American Chief Sealth. Only the settlers kind of morphed Sealth into Seattle," Angela said.

A grin lit up Mindy's face. "See, Angie? If you just concentrate, you know this stuff."

She bent back to studying the text on her monitor. "Let's keep going. There's always an essay at the end of the question part of the test, so keep an eye out for something really cool that you can write about..."

Chapter 6

Nana Ree had returned. Grilled cheese sandwiches had been made and eaten.

Teeth had been brushed, books had been closed, and laptops turned off.

Angela waited.

It was dark and quiet. Mindy's breathing was slow and steady.

Angela unrolled from the sleeping bag Mindy had loaned her. She hadn't changed into nightclothes. All she had to do was pick up her sneakers, slip her phone into a pocket, and grab her wallet out of her backpack.

Angela crept out of the bedroom and down the hall.

She paused outside Nana Ree's room, but heard only the soft, muffled snore of someone deep in sleep.

Angela decided taking the elevator was too noisy. It might wake Nana Ree.

So she tiptoed down the worn, wooden stairs.

At the bottom, she slipped on her shoes and stepped out into the Seattle night.

Chapter 7

It wasn't raining the way it had been last time.

The shop was across the street and down the block a little way. Angela could see the faint buzz-and-flicker of the neon green eye in the shop window.

There were a few people strolling the neighborhood, but no one paid Angela any mind.

She stepped out into the street and made her way toward the neon eye.

Stopping at the store window, Angela frowned as she looked at the name printed below the green eye...

What You Need

...was printed in curling, golden script.

Angela could have sworn it had said something completely different the last time she was here.

But the whole experience had been so weird.

Maybe I was in shock and don't remember things the way they really were? she thought. *Maybe...*

She fished her phone out of her pocket.

Angela snapped a picture. She also checked the phone's power and was pleased to see it was at 95%.

She also checked the old watch she wore. It had been her grandmother's. It was ticking along faithfully. It said 3 A.M.

Well, this time I know for sure that everything's working, Angela thought.

Feeling as prepared as she could be, she peeked through the shop's window and past the bead curtain hanging inside it. There didn't seem to be anyone moving around.

Angela grasped the brass doorknob, opened it, and stepped into the shop.

Chapter 8

She paused and closed her eyes, breathing deep and listening. There were no sounds other than the nighttime noises of any large city.

Her nose twitched. She could smell sage, strawberries, woodsmoke and… the ocean? It was a slightly different odor than the last time Angela had visited. It was fresher and more distinctly Seattle, she thought. But it still made her cough.

Angela muffled the sound as best she could. Her eyes darted from corner to dark corner, searching for movement.

Nothing.

Reassured that she was alone, Angela pulled

the street door closed behind her. She moved toward the familiar, dim glow coming from the very
back of the shop.

Where another door waited.

Nothing had changed.

The wooden door with the barely-visible carv-
ings was still there. Its doorknob was glistening
like an invitation.

Angela had thought it would be easier the second time. It wasn't.

I should have told someone where I was going.

She rested her fingers on the crystal doorknob
for a moment.

*What if something happens to me? What if I
can't get home this time? No one will know where
to look for me!*

Angela gripped the knob and turned it.

She was back at Pike Place Market. And it
was the dead of night.

Chapter 9

Angela stepped through the door. For a moment, she held her breath.

She concentrated on her surroundings. She used all her senses to figure out what was the same and what was different.

The wide staircase in front of her led downward, as expected.

But the pearl-green mist she remembered from her last visit was pinkish this time. It looked like the rosy hue that might be found inside a seashell.

It still curled and beckoned like last time. The mist formed cloud-like shapes.

The shapes might have been ghosts. Or might have been nothing at all.

The sound that danced on the fringes of Angela's hearing wasn't the same as last time, either.

Last time, she had heard music box chimes. This time, she thought it might be very, very distant drums or chanting.

She felt it in her bones more than she heard it.

The incense she'd smelled when she first entered the shop was deeper. Less strawberries. More woodsy. More sea-salty.

Angela decided it was a less pretty place than last time. It was more...

...*Primal!* she thought. *That's what it is. Like the ocean and the woods are taking over. Like life is older here. Weird.*

It was different enough to be a little scary.

With her heart pounding, Angela followed the seashell-pink mist that motioned her down the stairs.

Chapter 10

At the bottom, she held her breath.

She turned her head to look where Adam Zimmerman's Rewind Shop had been the last time she had visited.

Angela exhaled in a whoosh of pure relief.

The Rewind Shop was still there.

That one little bit of something familiar made all the difference in the world.

Even better, she could see Adam Zimmerman. He was standing behind his counter at the back of the store.

He was deep in discussion with a customer. Judging by Mr. Zimmerman's lively gestures, Angela thought it might be a spirited bit of bargaining.

She'd brought her wallet with the intention of paying for the little bottle Mr. Zimmerman had given her last time.

It had helped her get home that first time she was in the Market at night.

But Angela wasn't sure about interrupting what looked like serious business.

She stood uncertainly in the doorway of the Rewind Shop, hoping for a break in the conversation.

Chapter 11

Mr. Zimmerman's hair and beard went through two cycles of getting older... then getting younger... then getting older again before the Rewind Shop owner noticed Angela.

He waved and beamed a great smile. Angela took it as permission to come closer.

She overheard the end of Mr. Zimmerman's conversation with his customer.

"You must trust me, sir. All you need is Take A Step Back for your situation. You certainly don't require All The Time In The World! Trust me!" he repeated with force.

The customer mumbled something Angela couldn't hear. He fished a small, velvet pouch out of his coat pocket. He shook two golden coins onto the countertop.

Looking very sour indeed, he took the bottle Mr. Zimmerman held out to him. He stalked out of the Rewind Shop. He ignored Angela completely, pushing past her on his way to the door.

After the customer had disappeared into the pearly pink mist, Mr. Zimmerman threw his arms wide and boomed a happy greeting.

"Well, young lady! You've come back! I knew you would." He leaned closer and peered at Angela. "So you made it home without trouble, yes? I knew you would!"

Mr. Zimmerman seemed to already know the answers to his own questions. So Angela just smiled back at him as he continued talking.

"Now, what are you in the Market for tonight, young lady?" Adam Zimmerman's eyebrows rose and he chuckled. "That has two meanings, you know! 'In the market' as in what are you shopping for? And 'in the Market' as in here! This location! Pike Place Market!"

Angela watched silvery hairs thread through Mr. Zimmerman's beard and hair.

She was lost for a moment in the nonstop changes from old to young to old.

She remembered herself when Mr. Zimmerman cleared his throat and leaned a little closer.

He was waiting for an answer.

Chapter 12

Angela tore her eyes away from the waves of age and youth.

"I... I just came back to thank you and, uh, to pay you for last time... I think."

The last customer's coins were still on the counter. They looked like pure gold.

Angela wasn't sure she had enough money. Or the right kind of money.

And how did one put a price on magic, anyway?

"Pay? Pay!" Adam Zimmerman's head cocked to one side, his brows rising. "Oh, young lady... No. No, no, no, no, no. I don't want payment. I enjoyed meeting a Market newcomer. I was patting myself on the back for the rest of the night for having done a good deed. I helped a young lady get home! But..."

A thoughtful look came into Mr. Zimmerman's eyes.

"Come to think of it, there is something you can do for me..." He peered down at Angela. "Would you deliver a message for me? Could you do that? Of course you can! I knew you could!"

Angela was amused. And a little breathless. And more than a little concerned about exactly where she would have to go at this time of night to deliver a message.

Chapter 13

Adam Zimmerman bent low and rummaged about behind his counter.

After much rumbling and grumbling, he stood up. He waved a folded square of paper over his head like a trophy.

"Got it! Here you go, young lady."
He handed the little square of folded paper to Angela.

"I would consider it a great favor if you would take this and put it in the hand of Serenity Sanchez. Will you do that?"

Angela took the message, but blinked in confusion. "I... I mean...How... uh... Where..."

"Oh, my dear, I'm so sorry!" Adam Zimmerman slapped the palm of one hand against his forehead. "I keep forgetting you're a Market new-comer! Well, not to worry. Serenity is the owner of Dreamtime Books."

"What... Dreamtime Books?" Angela blinked, trying to remember all the bookstores in the Market.

She couldn't recall any named Dreamtime.

Then again, there was no Rewind Shop in the daytime Market, either.

She supposed it didn't mean much if she could only think of daytime stores. And she did owe Mr. Zimmerman for his help last time.

"Yes! Dreamtime Books! Yes!" Adam Zimmer-man nodded and gestured toward the door of his shop. "Turn left when you leave here and it's just 'round the corner. Can't miss it. And tell Serenity I sent you? Can you do that? I knew you could!"

Mr. Zimmerman clapped his hands together and beamed at Angela.

He had so much confidence in her. She couldn't argue back. At least, not without dashing his hopes and erasing the happy smile from his ever-changing face.

So Angela left Adam Zimmerman's Rewind Shop, note in hand. Angela did as she'd been told. She turned left.

And that's where things got confusing.

Chapter 14

It was the mist.

The shimmering, seashell-rosy mist. It moved with a purpose, not just from drafts and breezes.

As Angela walked, the mist gathered and swirled.

It hid some shops from view. It gave brief, teasing glimpses of others. But the only really clear view it allowed was a few feet of space directly in front of Angela's feet.

Angela felt she was being guided someplace.

She decided it wouldn't hurt to go along. After all, it seemed to be in the direction Mr. Zimmerman had wanted her to go.

But it was a little unsettling to see almost-shapes like almost-people and almost-things moving around her. It made her nervous and uncomfortable.

Angela couldn't tell if they were actual, solid things or if the mist was forming itself into likenesses of things, like clouds.

And every once in a while, some of the mist would come together, like a cotton ball. It would turn red.

The red cotton-ball mist would seem to follow Angela for a few steps. Then it would spread back out and turn pale pink again.

After what seemed like a longer time than it should have taken, the shimmering parted to reveal a sign.

Dreamtime Books
Serenity Sanchez, proprietor

Chapter 15

Angela stepped up to the store window and looked at the display. There were books of all sizes.

Huge coffee-table books.

Tiny books that were meant to fit in one's pocket.

They were stacked in towers that leaned.

They were scattered about, some lying open.

Some had pages that were turning on their own!

Angela shaded her eyes with one hand and peered deeper into the shop.

Shelves of books lined the walls from floor to ceiling. The center of the store was filled with pillows and cushions and quilts and comforters.

Angela stared at a mound of velvety-soft pillows the color of pale, dusty green. She felt her eyelids droop.

Normally, she'd be asleep at this hour. She leaned her forehead against the windowpane.

Just for a minute. Just to rest her eyes...

Angela startled awake, her eyes flying open.

A withered, wrinkled hand rested on her shoulder.

When she turned to see who was standing behind her, Angela thought she'd never seen any-one so ancient.

Even when Adam Zimmerman was at the oldest of his old-to-young-to-old cycle, he wasn't this old.

Angela stared. She couldn't help it, even though she knew staring was rude.

Chapter 16

The hand on Angela's shoulder belonged to a woman whose skin was creased and folded.

She had obviously lived a long, full life.

Angela noticed she wore a red bandana tied over her graying hair. The rest of her clothes were drab and rustic and forgettable. The bandana was bright in comparison.

The woman's bark-brown, weathered face rearranged itself into something like a smile.

She took a step back and nodded. She looked deeply into Angela's eyes.

Her lips moved, but Angela didn't hear anything.

"What? I'm sorry. I didn't hear you."

Angela moved closer. The old woman took another step backward. She stepped into the ever-present mist.

But the faint whisper of a word lingered.

Angeline.

Angela had to squint to see her. The woman was fading with each step. The rose-hued mist was curling around her, claiming her.

Angeline.

"No. My name's Angela."

Angeline.

The word ghosted out of the mist that had thickened to fog.

The last trace of the woman, her bright red bandana, seemed to break apart and become nothing more than mist itself.

The deep red paled and merged with the other twisting shapes of fragile pearly-pink.

She was gone.

Chapter 17

Angela didn't feel sleepy anymore.

She shivered as she turned her back on the shimmering fog where the old woman had disappeared.

She didn't waste another minute looking in windows. Angela opened the door to Dreamtime Books and stepped into the shop. Instantly, she felt safer.

Warm, golden light made the piles of pillows and cushions seem even softer and more inviting. The books looked inviting, too.

Angela would have liked nothing better than to curl up with one and rest for just a moment.

But she was on a mission.

She had to find Serenity Sanchez and give her the message from Mr. Zimmerman.

Angela walked further into the bookstore.

She gasped.

There were people nestled deep among some of the piles of cushions. She hadn't noticed them at first because they were so still.

They were asleep!

Angela took a cautious step closer and peered at the nests of pillows and the people snuggled in them.

She counted seven.

They ranged in age from early teens to middle-aged adults.

There were both men and women, boys and girls.

The only thing they all had in common was that each seemed to have fallen asleep while reading. Everyone had an open book resting against their chests.

And each had a faint, blissful smile.

"May I help you?"

Chapter 18

Angela jumped even though the words were spoken in a soft, hushed voice.

It was a voice that didn't want to wake anyone up.

It was an after-hours voice. A voice that belonged in a library.

When Angela turned and saw the speaker, she couldn't help grinning.

The woman was short, with raven-black hair braided into an elaborate crown. Tucked among the dark strands were what Angela thought were ornaments.

Until she realized they were moving.

Tiny, silvery buds sparkled in the woman's hair. As Angela watched, they opened, blossoming into golden flowers like fairy-buttercups.

After a moment or two, the golden flowers curled back into silver buds. Then they would repeat the process again and again.

The effect was enchanting.

Angela wondered if all the people who worked in the Market at night had something about them that was ever-changing.

Mr. Zimmerman with his age, and this person with her hair-flowers.

Apparently the woman was used to customers being distracted by her hair.

She waited patiently, smiling slightly, until Angela came back to herself. She'd been asked a question!

"Oh! Sorry!"

Angela looked away from the woman's hair. She looked at the people half-buried among pillows. She looked at the folded square of paper in her own hand.

She decided she had too many questions to ask. She needed to remember that she was running an errand.

Running an errand for a man who'd been very kind to her when she needed help.

She held the message she was carrying a little higher.

"I'm looking for the owner, I think. Serenity Sanchez? I'm supposed to give her this."

Chapter 19

The woman's brows rose. She tilted her head to one side and considered the paper.

"Indeed! Hmmm…"

She studied the note in Angela's hand. She didn't make a move to take it. She didn't tell Angela where she might find Serenity Sanchez.

The flowers blooming and closing in her hair started shifting faster. The woman turned on her heel and headed toward the back of the store. She motioned for Angela to follow.

The woman led Angela through a rickety door and behind a deep red velvet curtain embroidered with yellow roses.

They ended up in a small room with a desk, a

chair, and a lamp. The lamp had an elaborately beaded lampshade.

She gestured toward the desktop. Angela took it to mean she should put the message there.

But Mr. Zimmerman had been very clear. He wanted Angela to make sure it got to Serenity Sanchez herself.

Angela felt honor-bound to keep hold of the folded square of paper. She owed it to Mr. Zimmerman.

The little woman seemed to expect to be obeyed. When Angela didn't, she put her hands on her hips and began tapping her shoe.

It was a clear sign her patience was wearing thin.

Chapter 20

"I'm sorry," Angela said, "but I need to find the owner of the store. I can't give the message to anyone else. I'm sorry," she repeated.

"Oh, for heaven's sake... I am the owner," the woman said. Her eyes flashed. The flowers in her hair got even faster. "I'm Serenity Sanchez and I'm asking you to place that packet of unknown content on my desk."

"Unknown?" Angela gave the folded square of paper a puzzled look before setting it on the desktop. "It's just a message."

"Just a message?" Ms. Sanchez let her head droop and her eyes close for a moment. Her expression spoke of her long-suffering dealings with such ignorance. "'Just a message,' the girl says. Just a message."

She raised her head, straightened her shoulders, and looked at Angela with eyes that sparked fierce energy.

"My dear, do you know what one of the most powerful inventions in the world, maybe the entire universe, is? Do you?"

Angela wasn't sure she knew much of anything in this nighttime Market.

Regular rules and natural laws didn't seem to matter here. But she did recall her last visit with Adam Zimmerman.

He told her what the most precious substance in the world was. Angela wondered if maybe it was also the most powerful.

So she said, in a not-quite-sure little voice, "Time? Is it... time?"

Chapter 21

"What? No! Of course not!"

Serenity Sanchez seemed to take offense at such an idea. Angela had no idea why.

"It's words, my girl! Words! Why, what else can declare wars, bring peace, hurt and heal all at once?

"What else inspires whole civilizations, yet can wound like an arrow?

"What else is the basis of shared experiences and emotions that can span distance and time?

"Words! Words! And with so much power, words can be dangerous indeed!"

Angela looked down at the seemingly innocent folded square of paper with new respect.

She frowned. "Why would Mr. Zimmerman send you anything dangerous? He doesn't seem like that kind of man to me."

"Ah, but that's the thing about words, my dear. They can come off as something entirely different from what the person who wrote or said them intended! Yes," Serenity Sanchez said, crossing her arms and nodding sagely, "words are tricky little things."

"Well, I'm sure he didn't mean any harm, whatever the message is. Shall I open it for you?"

Angela only meant to be helpful, but Serenity gasped and shot an arm out. Her palm was toward Angela in the universal gesture that meant STOP! NO!

"Certainly not! You said the message was meant for me. Words can do a great deal of damage if they fall into the wrong hands!"

The blossoms in Ms. Sanchez's hair seemed to be opening and closing at a calmer pace.

She still didn't move toward the note on the desk, though.

Chapter 22

Angela shifted her weight from foot to foot. The owner of Dreamtime Books didn't take notice of her unease.

After a few more minutes, Angela sighed. She clearly wasn't any help in the drama of the message.

"Well," she finally said, "I'll leave you to it, then. Do you mind if I look around your store? I won't... um... wake any of your customers."

Serenity grunted, eyes fixed on the paper lying on her desktop.

"It's a store. You're supposed to look around. And you can't wake anyone up until they're done."

That didn't make any sense at all to Angela,

but she was grateful for the opportunity to return to the shelves and books in the store's main room.

There were books on every subject Angela could imagine, and some she would never have. She raised an eyebrow at whole sections devoted to *Poetry By And About Clams*, *Thimble Art*, *Egg-shell Embroidery*, and other topics she'd never thought existed.

Finally, she saw something more familiar. A shelf labeled *Local History* caught her eye.

Angela was drawn to it.

Chapter 23

She felt a little guilty about the study session with Mindy.

Angela knew she hadn't been giving her best effort. Her mind had been on getting to the Market instead of preparing schoolwork.

And now, it was a school night and she was out running around strange places and meeting strange people.

She would be sleepy and dull-witted when they had to take the history test tomorrow.

Angela didn't think there was much she could do about it now.

She'd made her choice. She'd chosen the Market at night over school.

And Mindy had mentioned the essay that their history teacher, Ms. Warden, liked to assign at the end of each of her tests.

It was rumored that even if you missed most of the questions, if you wrote a really, really good essay, Ms. Warden would give you a good grade.

But Angela thought it was too late for her to come up with anything that impressive now.

And then... the title of a book caught her eye and made her gasp.

Princess Angeline.

Chapter 24

Angela stared at the title on the spine of the book. It looked very old.

She reached up and pried it loose. It was squeezed in between two other books. They had ordinary titles: *Old Seattle* and *Pacific Coast History.*

She coughed as a layer of dust drifted off of the book's cover. The ancient woman outside Dreamtime Books had whispered the word "Angeline." At least, it's what Angela thought she'd heard.

At the time, it had seemed like the woman had made a mistake and had gotten Angela's own name wrong.

Now, Angela wasn't so sure.

She opened the book's cover and looked for the date it had been published.

1898.

Angela had never seen a book so old. She wanted to find a comfortable place and read at least some of it.

What would a book written so long ago have to say?

She began to look for a place where she could read for a while.

The piles of pillows and quilts were inviting. Only she didn't want to disturb any of the people who were dozing with books lying open upon their chests.

Angela was considering a mound of forest green velvet cushions when she caught movement out of the corner of her eye.

She turned to see a young man. He looked just a few years older than she was. He was sitting up and stretching.

His book had fallen beside him in a tumble of pages. He yawned and then smiled when he saw Angela watching him.

Chapter 25

"Hi," the young man said.

"Hi," Angela replied.

The young man rose to his feet and stretched again. She glanced down at the fallen book.

Angela frowned. "Your book. The pages look… blank?"

"Huh?"

He bent low and retrieved the book from where it lay on a rumpled quilt. He flipped through the pages and gave a satisfied nod.

"Good. It worked." He looked back up at Angela. "It doesn't always, you know. Sometimes you have to give it a second go. But this…" He held the book high. "…This time, it did its job."

Angela looked confused.

The young man grinned. "I'm Kevin. Lemme guess… you're new and you've never done the dreamtime book thing before, right?"

Angela shook her head. "I don't even know what that means. I'm Angela, by the way. Nice to meet you."

Kevin's grin grew even wider. "So our Miss Serenity didn't explain how to use this place?"

Angela swept her gaze around the room, but didn't gain any knowledge from doing so.

"It's a bookstore," she said. "You buy books and read them."

Really, how many ways were there to use books?

Angela was about to learn a new one.

Chapter 26

Kevin stepped closer to Angela. "Here, let me show you something."

Angela took an involuntary step backwards when he began to loosen the top two buttons of his shirt.

Kevin chuckled and shook his head. "I just wanna show you what the books here do. Here. Look."

He pulled the collar of his shirt down and pointed to a chilly-looking white scar.

Angela bent closer and peered at it. Then she straightened and gave Kevin a puzzled look. "I don't get it."

Kevin began to fasten the buttons on his shirt, hiding the scar from view. "That's where the words entered in."

Angela's eyes widened. "Where the...
entered... words... where they... WHAT?"

"Kevin, stop it. You're scaring the girl."

Serenity Sanchez had returned.

She had dealt with the message Angela had
delivered and was apparently ready to get back to
running Dreamtime Books.

"I'm just showing her!" Kevin protested his
innocence, but there was a twinkle in his eye. He
rather enjoyed mischief, too.

"Well, I'll take over now. Thank you. You can
get on with your own studies." Serenity dismissed
the young man.

She turned her attention to Angela.

Chapter 27

This was a very different Serenity Sanchez than the one who'd been so suspicious and nervous about the message. So Angela asked, "Was the message okay? Not something, you know... dangerous?"

"Adam Zimmerman wrote that I should help you. That you would be needing something."

Angela blinked. "But... but... that message was already written. He didn't even know I was coming to the Market. I didn't even know for sure if I was coming here!"

Serenity shrugged. "In matters of 'when,' in matters of time, Adam lives by his own rules. Anyway, I see you have selected the book you need."

Angela looked down at the cover with its blocky, rustic-looking letters... *Princess Angeline.* She ran her palm over the title and shook her head. "I don't know if I need this or not, but something weird happened right before I came in here. There was this woman..."

"Ah. Red kerchief over her hair? Very, very, extremely old?" Serenity interrupted.

Her slight smile looked as though she already knew the answers to Angela's question.

"Yes. Who is she?"

"It's better to ask who *was* she."

Chapter 28

"Was?" A creepy feeling coaxed the tiny hairs on the back of Angela's neck into a scared-and-shivery upright position.

Serenity's nose twitched with impatience.

"My dear, history is about the past. It's about what was. And about who was."

Serenity nodded at the book Angela was holding.

"The lady you met was Princess Angeline. She was. She is no longer. At least, not in the way ordinary folks can see and talk to her."

Angela swallowed what felt like a lump of ice in her throat. "You mean... she's... she was... I mean, now she's a... ghost?"

Serenity sighed. "Ghost. Spirit. I'm not sure quite what she is, but I have work to do.

"An actor, a Shakespearean actor, is coming in. I need to have the right books ready. He's on stage tomorrow, so he doesn't have time to learn his lines the regular way, you know.

"So, find a place to lie down and..."

The horrified, confused look on Angela's face made Serenity stop short.

"Goodness me. I keep forgetting you're a newbie."

Serenity placed a hand on Angela's back and steered her toward the pile of pillows Kevin had vacated.

"Here's how it works, my dear. Make yourself comfortable and start reading. The book will know what to do."

"What does that even mean?" Angela was looking panicked. "What was that scar Kevin showed me? I don't understand!"

"It's really quite simple as long as you do as you're told, my dear. Now, I really must go find a nice copy of Shakespeare's works for that poor actor."

Serenity had begun to walk away. She turned back with a sympathetic look.

"It'll be all right, my dear. Besides... Adam Zimmerman said you need this."

And with that, Serenity Sanchez, hair ornaments blossoming and closing and blossoming once more, disappeared deep into the shelves and stacks of Dreamtime Books.

Chapter 29

Angela settled herself among the velvet cushions. They were soft, and a deep midnight blue. It
should have been a relaxing color.

But Angela had ghosts and white scars and
riddles and mysteries running through her head.
How could she possibly relax?

Angela wondered how late it was getting. She
pulled her phone out of her pocket.
All she saw was a blank, dead screen.

"No! No, no, no, no, no! I charged you! I know
I did!"

With a sinking feeling, Angela pushed up the
sleeve of her jacket.

Her grandmother's watch was stylish and vintage. And it was frozen. The second hand was stopped dead.

Angela put her phone back in her pocket.

She slumped against the mounded pillows and thought about hugging one of them for comfort.

But the book *Princess Angeline* was already in her arms. She hugged the book instead and tried to talk herself out of panic.

It doesn't really matter what time it is, she told herself. *This time all I have to do is cross the street to Mindy's place. And if Mindy or Nana Ree are already awake, if they catch me coming in, I'll just say I was out for a walk.*

Angela told herself that wasn't really a lie. She would just be fudging the truth a little.

She told herself that her panic was from the shock of finding her phone and watch had stopped.

They'd done the same thing during her last visit to the night Market.

She'd made sure both were working before coming this time, but the same thing had happened.

It was just shock. It wasn't a panic-worthy problem this time.

After a while, her breathing was regular. Her heart wasn't pounding.

She really was curious about a book published in 1898.

Angela opened *Princess Angeline*.

Angela began to read.

Chapter 30

Princess Angeline was the oldest daughter of Chief Seattle, the Native American after whom Seattle was named…

Angela's eyes felt heavy. The book felt heavy, too. She nestled deeper into the velvet pillows.

Princess Angeline… Princess Angeline…

…But that wasn't always my name…

Angela didn't know where the voice was coming from, but it was so peaceful, so soft, so lulling…

Angela wasn't in Dreamtime Books anymore. In fact, she wasn't in the Market at all!

There were wooden buildings and houses scattered around a hillside that sloped down to the sea.

Angela could smell the familiar, salty scent of the ocean.

It was her first clue.

I'm in Seattle! And this... this is between Pike and Pine Streets, I think, but... they look so different!

The streets weren't paved. Some of the houses looked rough, as though they'd been made out of logs.

Some of the larger buildings were smoother-looking. Clearly they had been built after the more rough ones.

There were no crowds. A few people in odd clothes walked the dirt streets.

No cars. Some horses and wagons, though.

There was a voice. It was sad and distant, but right in her ear...

Chapter 31

I was born in 1820. My name was Kikisoblu. My father was a chief of the Duwamish tribe.

The voice told a tale of a chief. Chief Se'ahl. But settlers couldn't pronounce his name, so they called him Seattle.

His daughter, Kikisoblu, drew the attention of a pioneer wife. The woman decided she would bring her own religion to the girl.

Kikisoblu was christened in the Roman Catholic Church. She was renamed Angeline. And because her father was a chief, the settlers thought of him as local royalty.

Angeline became known as Princess Angeline.

The voice told Angela about how, around

1855, a treaty was enforced.

The U.S. government told all the Native Americans that they had to move from their homes. They were told to move to a reservation. But Princess Angeline refused.

She would not leave her home. She would stay on the piece of land she loved.

She would stay in her little waterfront cabin between Pike and Pine Streets.

The others were moved, relocated to a reservation.

Princess Angeline stayed.

She was alone. She was dignified and stubborn.

She felt these newcomers to the land had no right to tell anyone where to go.

After a while, people stopped asking Princess Angeline to move away. They began to respect her.

She became a familiar figure in Seattle. Everyone recognized her.

Then she became famous, although she didn't seem to know it. Photographers paid her for the privilege of her portrait.

She did some laundry to bring in money for what little she needed. She also got help from the very settlers who had once asked her to move.

A small grocery store near her cabin gave her free groceries. Others tried to make her lonely life easier.

Seattle's citizens now admired the proud attitude and bravery of Princess Angeline.

Through the years, she became known for the red bandana she almost always wore over her hair.

Princess Angeline grew old, as all must.

Seattle grew larger. Progress would not be denied.

But Princess Angeline stayed in her cabin and continued to live as she always had.

Alone.

She died on May 31st, 1896. She was laid to rest in a local cemetery.

Her coffin was crafted in the shape of a canoe.

The red bandana was no longer seen on the streets of Seattle. Princess Angeline's cabin was torn down. It was replaced with the beginnings of what would be Seattle's waterfront and Pike Place Market.

Chief Seattle's daughter tried to remain in the world of her own people, even as the modern world tried to push her out.

In the end, Princess Angeline was a woman caught between worlds.

And I still am... the voice murmured.

Chapter 32

Angela startled awake, the voice still whispering in her ear.

I still am caught between worlds… I still am…

Goosebumps prickled Angela's arms and neck. She sat up, expecting to see unpaved streets and wooden buildings. She looked for people in rustic clothing and for horses and buggies.

It was all so clear in her mind. If she tried, she could see every detail, hear every word of Princess Angeline's story.

But that world of long ago, the world told of in a book published in 1898, was gone.

All Angela saw were shelves of books and a great many pillows and quilts.

She inhaled deeply and then let her breath out in a slow, steady stream. It helped calm her. It helped let her get her bearings.

Angela looked down at the book *Princess Angeline*. It had been lying against her chest. When she had sat up, it had fallen into her lap. She opened it with trembling hands.

The pages were blank.

There was nothing printed on them. Not even the publication date: 1898.

Angela dropped the book. For a moment, she did nothing but stare at it.

Then, very, very slowly, she pulled down the neckline of her t-shirt.

A small, icy-white scar rested just under her collarbone.

Chapter 33

"Ah. All done, I see."

Serenity Sanchez bustled by, arms full of books. Her hair blossoms were opening and closing.

Angela raised her gaze from her new scar.

"What... what happened? What did you do to me?"

"Do to you? Why, nothing, my girl!" Serenity shook her head and smiled. "Sometimes it's easier to let things take their course than to try and explain them. Especially if you know that no harm will come of doing so."

"I don't understand," said Angela.

"Adam Zimmerman sent me a note asking me to do him a favor. He said the bearer of the note would be needing something. He would be very pleased if I let you have some dream-time with whichever book you chose." Serenity shrugged. "So, I did."

Angela thought this must be what being in shock felt like.

She closed her eyes and concentrated on breathing long, slow breaths.

Serenity continued on her way, putting books back on shelves and humming to herself.

After a few minutes, Angela felt better. But there was still a lot for her to puzzle out.

She stood and made her way to the door of Dreamtime Books. She waited for a moment, hand on the doorknob, but decided it was time to go home.

Angela left the shop and stepped into the swirls of rose-colored mist. She made sure she turned right, so she wouldn't get lost.

She was retracing her steps back toward Adam Zimmerman's Rewind Shop.

And thinking of Mr. Zimmerman made Angela stop in her tracks.

Chapter 34

He looked through time somehow. That's what he does.

He sent me to a place he thought I needed to go.

A slow grin began to spread across Angela's face.

She'd risked doing poorly in tomorrow's history test just so she could visit the Market at night. The best way she could do well at this point was to write a really good essay at the end of the test.

Angela closed her eyes again, doing a test of her own.

Yes, it's all still with me… or in me… or… something. I can still hear Princess Angeline if I try.

Angela opened her eyes. She couldn't decide exactly how she felt.

But she did know that she could now write a killer essay about local Seattle history. It would be about how Seattle's "heart," the Pike Place Market, was built where the daughter of a chief had once lived.

It was perfect.

It was what she needed to pass the history test.

Chapter 35

Angela made her way to the Rewind Shop through the mist. From time to time, she thought she could see a red bandana out of the corner of her eye.

It might have been the pink mist playing tricks of its own.

Or it might have been a woman trapped between two worlds who almost shared a name with Angela.

Angela reached the bottom of the stairs. They would take her up to the street and back to Mindy's and Nana Ree's place.

First, she paused to look into the Rewind Shop.

Mr. Zimmerman was leaning against the doorjamb, just inside the store. A truly huge grin beamed from his ever-changing, old-to-young-to-old face.

"Did you find what you needed, young lady?"

Adam Zimmerman's jolly voice boomed through the arcade.

Angela could only nod and smile in return.

"I knew you would!"

Chapter 36

Angela passed her history test.

Once she didn't need the knowledge anymore, the ice-white scar faded away.

But Angela never forgot Princess Angeline and what a brave but lonely life she'd lived in old Seattle.

Angela wondered what other secrets Pike Place Market might have.

There was only one way to find out.

Angela would need to visit the Market again.

At night.

About the Author

Cat Jenkins lives in the Pacific Northwest where the weather is often conducive to long hours before a keyboard. Her stories in humor, fantasy, speculative fiction, and horror have been published both online and in print. Her first novel, Sara When She Chooses, was published by Bedazzled Ink Publishing in May 2018. Cat's blog can be found at: catjenkinsdotcom.wordpress.com.

About the Publisher

Storyshares is a publisher focused on supporting the millions of teens and adults who struggle with reading by creating a new shelf in the library specifically for them. The ever-growing collection features content that is compelling and culturally relevant for teens and adults, yet still readable at a range of lower reading levels.

Storyshares generates content by engaging deeply with writers, bringing together a community to create this new kind of book. With more intriguing and approachable stories to choose from, the teens and adults who have fallen behind are improving their skills and beginning to discover the joy of reading. For more information, visit storyshares.org.

Easy to read. Hard to put down.